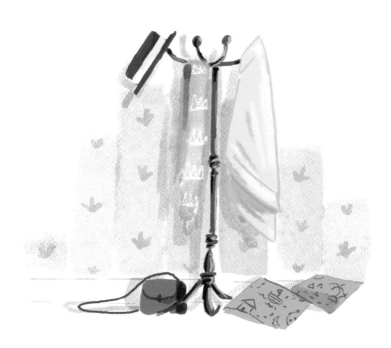

Dedicated to the brave Marcello.

BUSHEL
& PECK
BOOKS

Text copyright © 2022 by J. Donnini
Illustration copyright © 2022 by Luke Scriven

Published by Bushel & Peck Books, a family-run publishing house in Fresno, California, that
believes in uplifting children with the highest standards of art, music, literature, and ideas.
Find beautiful books for gifted young minds at www.bushelandpeckbooks.com.

Type set in Providence Sans, Mathlete, and Zooja Pro

Bushel & Peck Books is dedicated to fighting illiteracy all over the world. For every book we
sell, we donate one to a child in need—book for book. To nominate a school or organization to
receive free books, please visit www.bushelandpeckbooks.com.

LCCN: 2021951281
ISBN: 9781638190899

First Edition

Printed in China

10 9 8 7 6 5 4 3 2 1

This Will Pass

J. DONNINI

Illustrated by LUKE SCRIVEN

It was a special day for Crue,
and he buzzed with excitement.

An important guest was about to arrive . . . a guest who always brought the *best* presents. This year, Crue had been promised a great, big surprise.

KNOCK, KNOCK, KNOCK!

The door flew open, and in he danced. "YOUR GREAT-UNCLE OLLIE IS HERE!"

Ollie was Crue's favorite uncle. He was an adventurer who sailed the wild seas.

"Tomorrow," announced Great-Uncle Ollie, "we sail to the island of Mashore! It is time for you to see more of the wonders of this magical world."

Crue was thrilled, but then he began to worry. After all, this was a very

BIG JOURNEY!

What if the boat broke...

. . . or an octopus swallowed them up in one gulp . . .

. . . or a family of whales took over the boat?

But Crue trusted Great-Uncle Ollie, so he decided to go. The next day, they set sail on their adventure.

The boat sailed smoothly for the first few days. They played checkers and chess and lounged on the waves playing catch until dark.

But one night before bed,
a dark cloud crept in.

The waves CRASHED and SWIRLED, spinning the boat like a top. Crue shut his eyes tight and squeezed his uncle's hand.

"BE CALM, IT WILL PASS," said Great-Uncle Ollie. "This happens a lot at sea, young Crue. It feels scary when the boat seems out of control. If you take slow, deep breaths and stay calm, you will see that very soon the storm will be gone."

Great-Uncle Ollie held Crue and began to sing:

"Be calm, it will pass,
be calm, it will pass."

Over and over, he sang
through the night:

"Be calm, it will pass,
be calm, it will pass,"
until, finally, they drifted
off to sleep.

"BE CALM, IT WILL PASS."

When morning came, Great-Uncle Ollie was right: the storm was gone, and the sun had come out. But there were more adventures to come.

Some were FUN and EXCITING!

Some made Crue feel very SCARED.

...and SEA PIRATES who tried to take over the boat!

"BE CALM, IT WILL PASS."

But with each frightening event, Crue started to realize that Great-Uncle Ollie was right: every time, it *did* pass. Yes, Crue was scared. But when he slowed down his breath and he sang the words, he began to trust that everything would be okay.

After many weeks at sea, Crue and
Great-Uncle Ollie finally reached land.

They built
sandcastles . . .

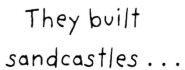

. . . and fell asleep
under coconut trees.

But one day, Great-Uncle Ollie said, "Crue, it's now time to go. You must sail with my shipmates back to your home."

"But Uncle Ollie, aren't you coming too?" asked Crue.

"No," he said, "this was to be my last trip. Here I will live and here I will stay. But when you go, remember my words, because there will always be problems and storms. 'Be calm, it will pass' helped us as we sailed, and it will help you when you're all by yourself."

Crue set sail, feeling brave and strong. He took Great-Uncle Ollie's words with him on his journey back home.

On his way home, Crue again faced many challenges:

More STORMS that he weathered . . .

. . . SHARKS that he fought . . .

...and SEA PIRATES, who he kicked right off the boat!

He took slow, deep breaths and sang the words, "Be calm, it will pass," and it always did.

Crue was now a brave sailor of the sea,
just like his Great-Uncle Ollie.

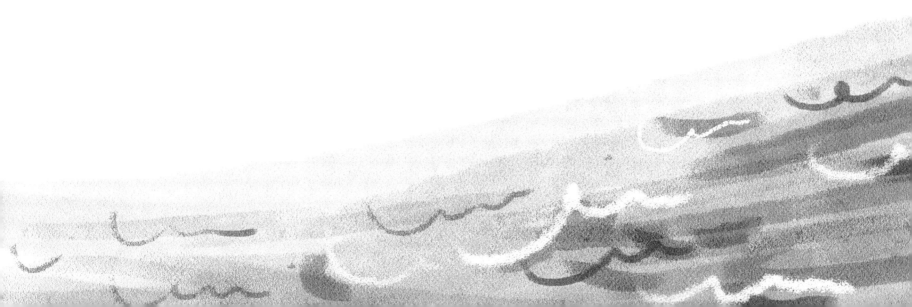

Tips for Parents

Many kids experience anxiety, and it can be difficult to know what to do. Here are two breathing techniques that can help; when you adjust your breathing, your mind and body will follow.

BREATHING EXERCISE

Do the following exercise using your belly to breathe. You should see your belly going out (breathing in) and in (breathing out) like a balloon. Your shoulders should not move. This takes practice, but you can do it!

- Close your mouth and inhale slowly through your nose to a mental count of four.
- Hold your breath for a count of seven.
- Exhale completely and slowly through your mouth, making a *whoosh* sound to a count of eight.
- Do this until you start to feel calm.

MANTRA

If you're feeling nervous or scared, you can try to sing a mantra or song like, "Be calm, it will pass" in your mind or out loud. As you sing "Be calm," inhale slowly and deeply, and as you sing, "it will pass," exhale slowly and deeply through pursed lips. The exhale breath should be longer than the inhale breath.

As with any mantra, you must believe the words you are saying. Remember, everything *does* pass!